skyscraper

Jorey Hurley

A Paula Wiseman Book
Simon & Schuster Books for Young Readers
New York London Toronto Sydney New Delhi

A STREET

ONE WAY

crush

scoop

dig

push

dump

drill

pour

stack

haul

raise

place

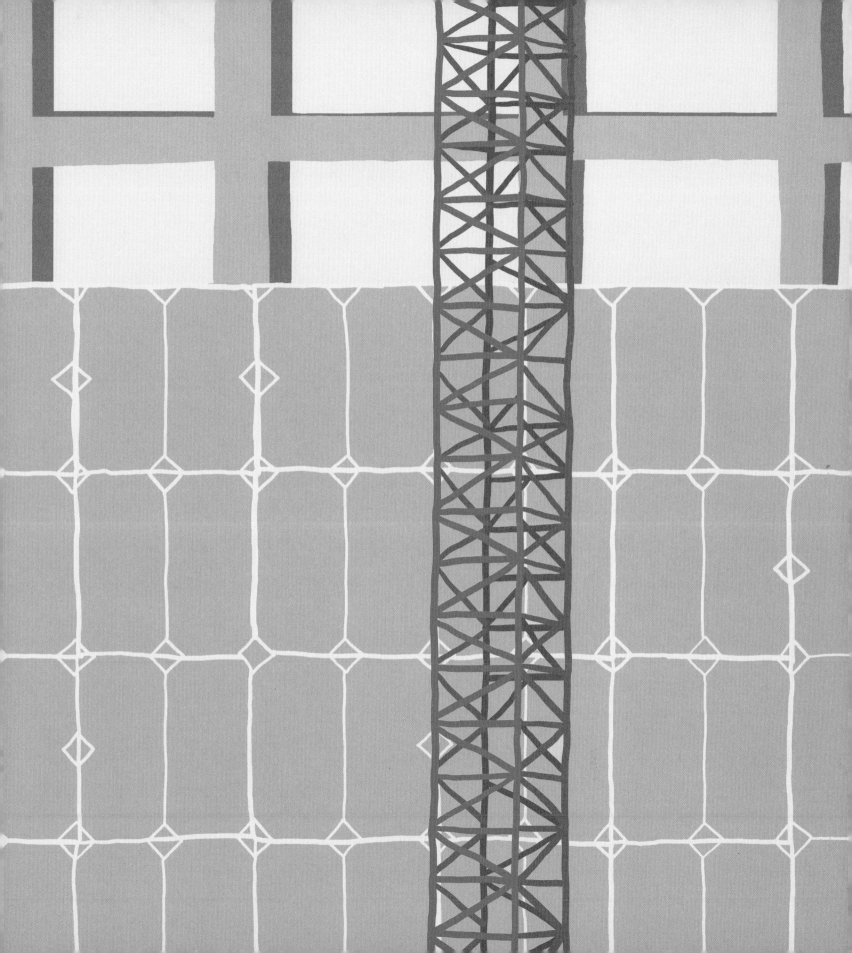

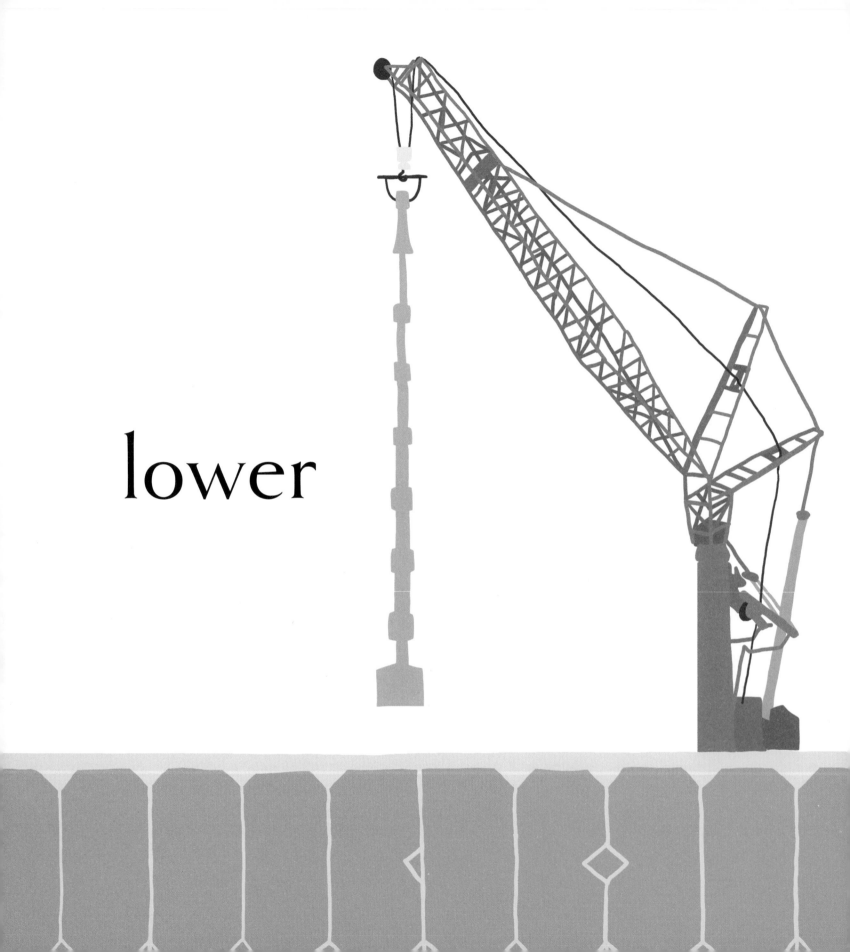

lower

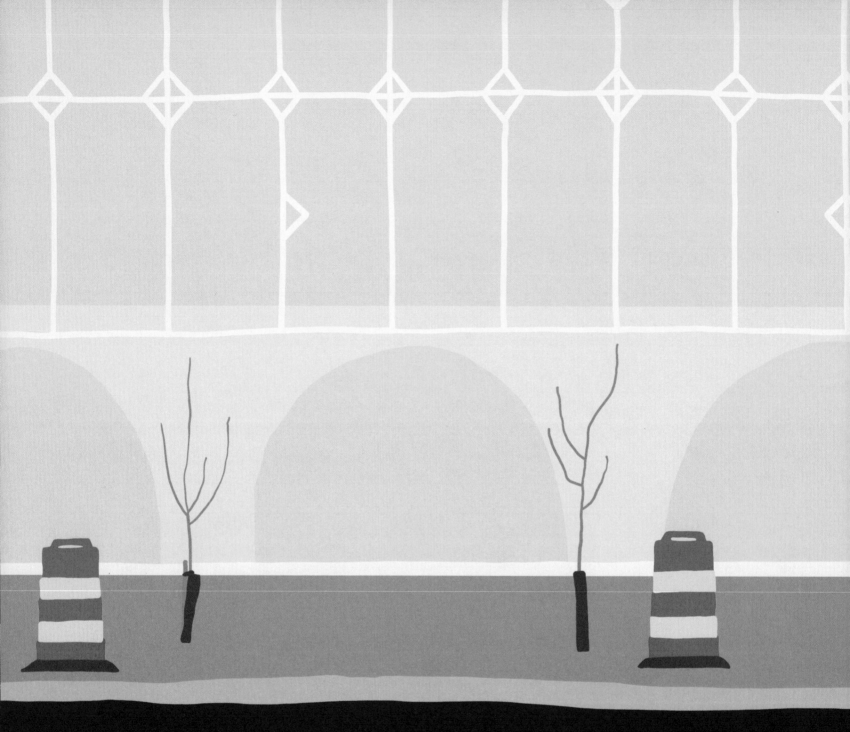

roll

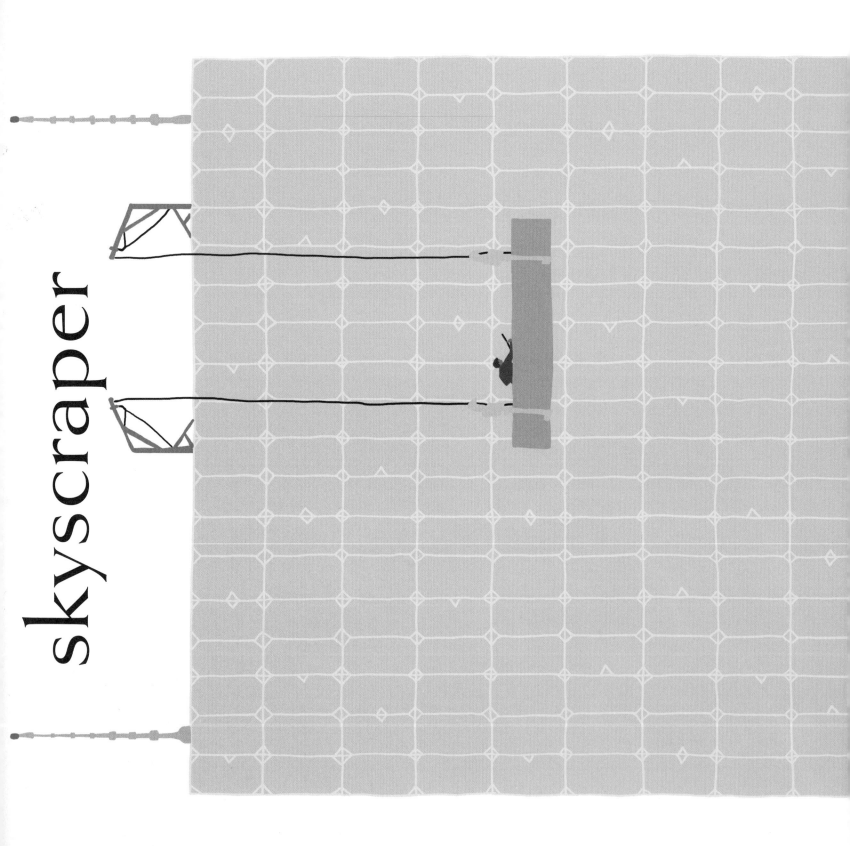

skyscraper

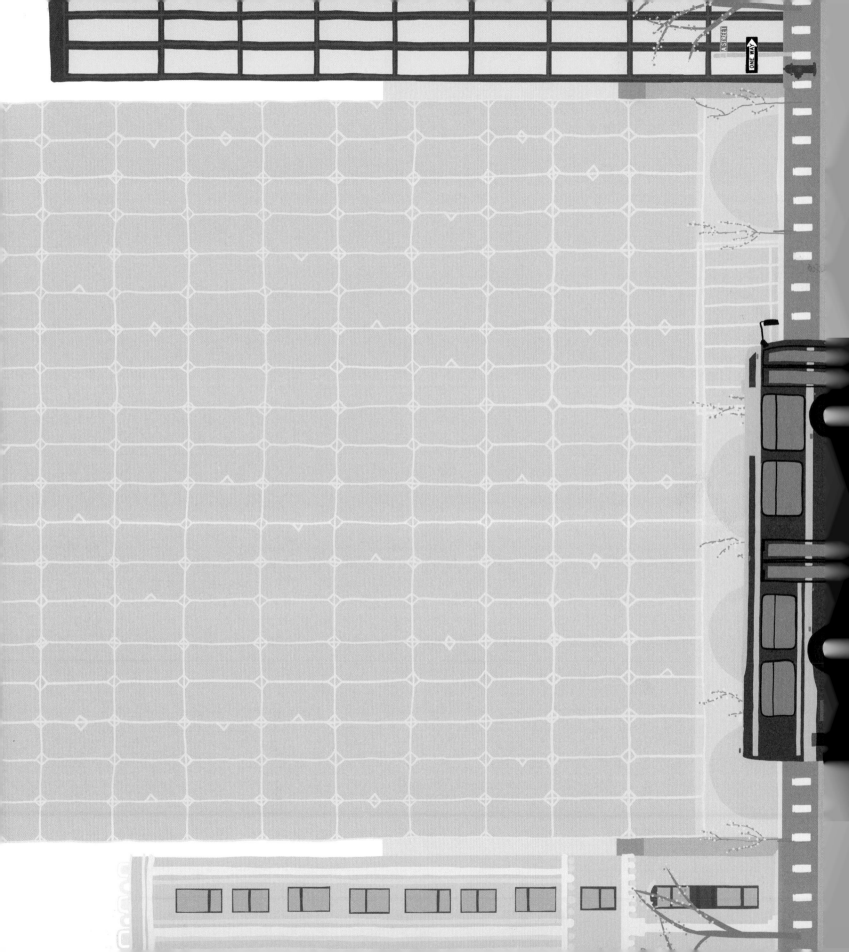

city

for little
builders
everywhere

SIMON & SCHUSTER BOOKS FOR YOUNG READERS • An imprint of Simon & Schuster Children's Publishing Division • 1230 Avenue of the Americas, New York, New York 10020 • Copyright © 2019 by Jorey Hurley • All rights reserved, including the right of reproduction in whole or in part in any form. • SIMON & SCHUSTER BOOKS FOR YOUNG READERS is a trademark of Simon & Schuster, Inc. • For information about special discounts for bulk purchases, please contact Simon & Schuster Special Sales at 1-866-506-1949 or business@simonandschuster.com. • The Simon & Schuster Speakers Bureau can bring authors to your live event. For more information or to book an event, contact the Simon & Schuster Speakers Bureau at 1-866-248-3049 or visit our website at www.simonspeakers.com. • Book design by Greg Stadnyk and Lizzy Bromley • The text for this book was set in Goldenbook. • The illustrations for this book were rendered in Photoshop. • Manufactured in China • 1118 SCP • First Edition • 10 9 8 7 6 5 4 3 2 1 • Library of Congress Cataloging-in-Publication Data • Names: Hurley, Jorey, author, illustrator. • Title: Skyscraper / Jorey Hurley. • Description: First edition. | New York : Simon & Schuster Books for Young Readers, [2019] | Audience: Age 4-8. | Audience: K to Grade 3. | "A Paula Wiseman Book." • Identifiers: LCCN 2018016737 | ISBN 9781481470018 (hardcover) | ISBN 9781481470025 (e-book) • Subjects: LCSH: Skyscrapers—Juvenile literature. • Classification: LCC NA6230 .H867 2019 | DDC 720/.483—dc23 LC record available at https://lccn.loc.gov/2018016737

glossary

1. A demolition excavator is used to demolish, or tear down, buildings. The claw attachment on the end of the movable arm here is called a grapple. The operator uses the grapple to grab or drag pieces off the building being demolished.

2. A front loader lifts and relocates batches of loose materials, such as demolition debris.

3. A hydraulic excavator digs trenches, holes, or building foundations. The arm that does the digging includes a boom (a long pole closest to the cab), a stick, and a bucket at the end.

4. A bulldozer pushes large amounts of dirt, gravel, or debris along the ground using a large metal plate called a blade. It moves on tracks, which help it grip the ground, even on very rough terrain, and spread its weight out more than wheels would, so it doesn't sink into muddy ground and get stuck.

5. A dump truck transports loose material, like sand, gravel, or demolition debris, in an open box called a load bed. Hydraulic pistons lift up the front end of the bed and the contents slide out through the hinged gate at the back.

6. A pile driver is used to drive piles (very large stakes) into the ground as part of the foundation that support a building. It lifts a heavy weight and then drops it down exactly on the top of the pile to drive it into the soil.

7. A concrete pump truck works with a concrete transport truck. Its chutes and hoses guide the still-liquid concrete directly to the place it is needed on the job site.

8. A concrete transport truck is made to transport concrete to the construction site while mixing it, which keeps it from hardening before it is poured into its final location. The truck keeps the concrete liquid by continuously spinning its drum, the large container on the back. Inside the drum is a corkscrew-like spiral blade that can spin in one direction to mix the concrete down into the drum and then spin in the other direction to force the concrete up and out of the drum.

9. A mobile crane is a crane mounted on tracks or tires to easily move around a job site. It has a telescoping (extendable) boom that stretches upward and supports and controls a wire rope running through pulleys, called sheaves, and suspending a hook.

10. A tractor-trailer, or semi truck, pulls a flatbed trailer loaded with steel beams, or other building materials that are not fragile or vulnerable to rain.

11. Tower cranes are used in the construction of very tall buildings. The base is fixed to a concrete slab and the vertical mast is often attached to the side of a building. The longer horizontal jib (the longer part of the crane) suspends the hook with the load, and the shorter counter jib carries a counterweight to balance against the load being lifted.

12. An aerial work platform, also known as a cherry picker, is a mobile piece of equipment that gives people and their equipment temporary access to high-up areas.

13. A luffing-jib crane has a very short counter jib, which allows it to rotate within a narrow radius. This makes it particularly useful in preventing crashes when multiple cranes are operating near each other.

14. A road roller is used to compact gravel, concrete, or asphalt in the construction of roads, which ensures that the final road surface is smooth.